Thumbelina

Retold by Margaret Nash

Illustrated by Sarah Horne

W

FRANKLIN WATTS
LONDON • SYDNEY

Thumbelina

First published in 2006 by
Franklin Watts
338 Euston Road
London
NW1 3BH

Franklin Watts Australia
Hachette Children's Books
Level 17/207 Kent Street
Sydney
NSW 2000

A CIP catalogue record for this book is available
from the British Library.

ISBN 0 7496 6580 7 (hbk)
ISBN 0 7496 6587 4 (pbk)

Series Editor: Jackie Hamley
Series Advisor: Dr Barrie Wade
Series Designer: Peter Scoulding

Printed in China

Long ago, there was
a beautiful girl as tiny
as your thumb.

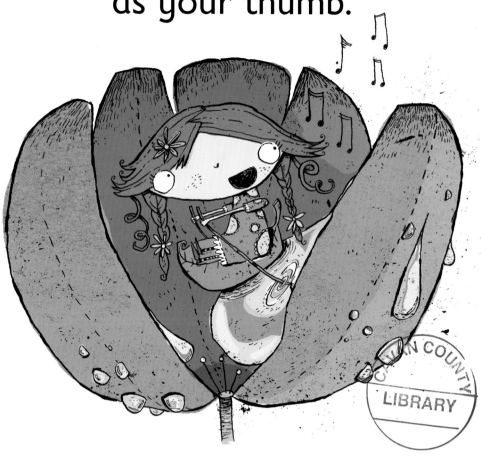

She was called Thumbelina.

One night, a toad stole her away and trapped her on a lily pad.

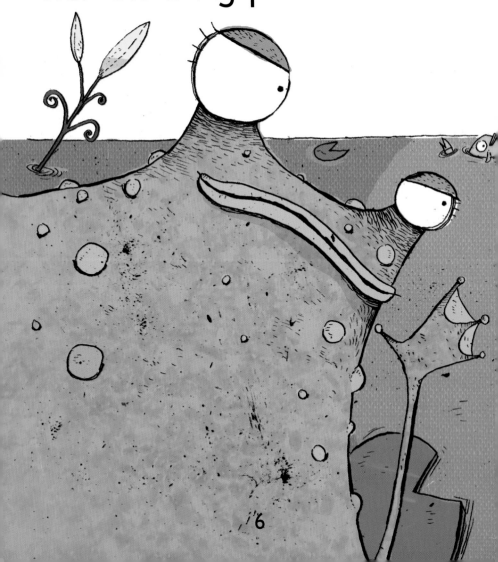

"You will marry my son!"
she said. Thumbelina cried
for the son was horrible.

A fish heard Thumbelina crying and nibbled the lily pad free.

Thumbelina floated away and a kind butterfly pulled her along.

Then a beetle swooped
down and grabbed
Thumbelina.

But the beetle's friends
thought she was ugly,
so he left her on a daisy.

All summer, Thumbelina listened happily to the birds singing sweetly.

But winter soon came
and Thumbelina started
to freeze.

A fieldmouse rescued her. "You can stay with me," she said, "but you must marry my friend, the mole. He lives underground."

The mole showed
Thumbelina a dead
swallow at the end
of his tunnel.

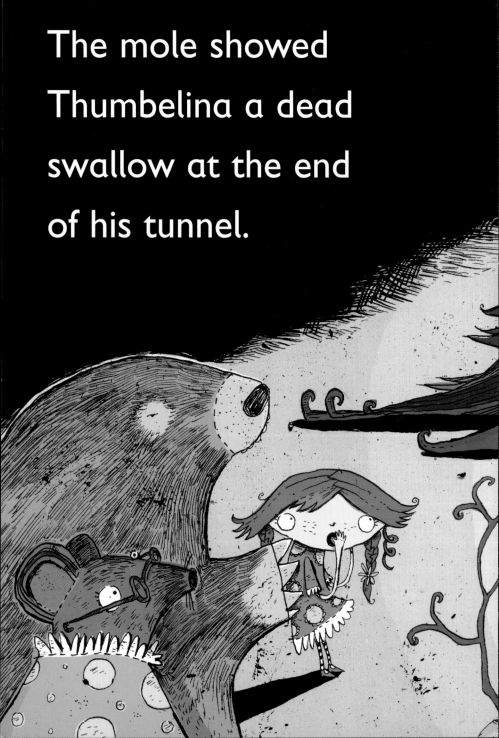

"Stupid bird!" he said,
as he kicked it.

Thumbelina kissed
the poor swallow.
"Thank you for singing
so sweetly last summer,"
she said.

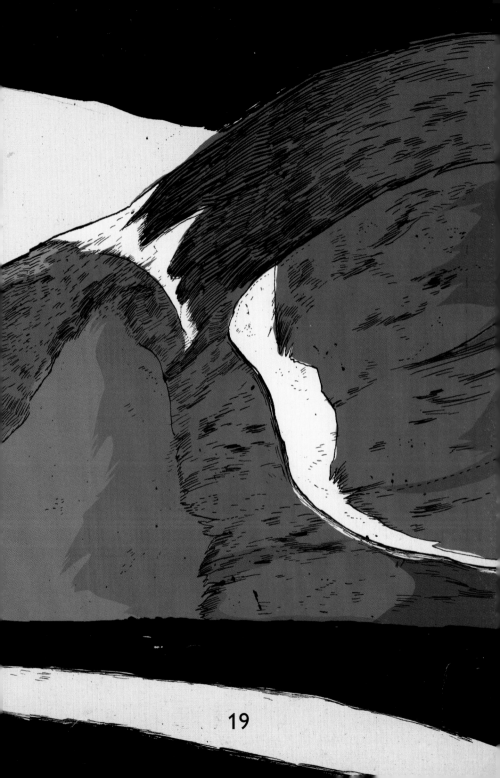

Thumbelina made
a blanket to cover
the swallow.

As she laid it over him, the swallow moved. He was alive, but his wing was torn!

Thumbelina nursed the swallow better until springtime.

"Thank you, but I must go soon," he said. "What will you do?"

"I must stay here,"
said Thumbelina sadly.
"The fieldmouse is
planning my wedding
to the miserable mole."

The day before her wedding, Thumbelina took a long, last look at the outside world.

She would live underground
from now on. Just then,
the swallow saw her and
flew down.

"Dear Thumbelina," he said. "Do come with me!" The swallow spread his wings, and Thumbelina climbed up.

They flew over fields ...

seas ...

and mountains.

Finally they landed in
the swallow's snug nest.
Thumbelina was safe
and happy at last.

Leapfrog has been specially designed to fit the requirements of the National Literacy Strategy. It offers real books for beginning readers by top authors and illustrators.

There are 49 Leapfrog stories to choose from:

* hardback